a Line of Duty novella

PROTECTING
What's Theirs

a Line of Duty novella

PROTECTING
What's Theirs

#1 *NEW YORK TIMES* BESTSELLING AUTHOR
TESSA BAILEY

This book is a work of fiction. Names, characters, places, and incidents are the product of the author's imagination or are used fictitiously. Any rtesemblance to actual events, locales, or persons, living or dead, is coincidental.

Copyright © 2014 by Tessa Bailey. All rights reserved, including the right to reproduce, distribute, or transmit in any form or by any means. For information regarding subsidiary rights, please contact the Publisher.

Entangled Publishing, LLC
644 Shrewsbury Commons Ave
STE 181
Shrewsbury, PA 17361
rights@entangledpublishing.com

Brazen is an imprint of Entangled Publishing, LLC.

Edited by Heather Howland
Cover design by LJ Anderson/Mayhem Cover Creations
Cover photography by VitalikRadko/DepositPhotos

Manufactured in the United States of America

First Edition March 2014

ENTANGLED
BRAZEN

For Bailey's Babes
"Get a Fan"

Chapter One

Shitshitshit.

Ginger Peet took one look at the offending piece of plastic in her hand and hurled it clear across the room. It was reflex. An unconscious action. If she'd have held it a second longer, it surely would have set her hand on fire. She watched the object bounce off her chest of drawers and slide to a stop at the base of her life-size Dolly Parton statue. For once, the giant porcelain likeness of her idol offered zero comfort, the Smoky Mountain Songbird's frozen smile taking on more of a smirking quality that Ginger definitely did not appreciate. Not now, when she'd just gotten the shock of a lifetime.

Considering some of the shocks she'd been dealt in her lifetime, especially in the last year, that was truly saying something.

"Well, Dolly?" Ginger plopped down hard on the wooden floor, the heels of her cowboy boots making a loud *clunk*. "No clever, down-home advice for me? You're just going to stand there and act all high and mighty? I didn't plan for this to happen, you know." She breathed a sigh. "I don't mean it,

Dolly. I'm just upset, is all."

Of course, the statue kept quiet, although when Ginger looked away for a split second, she swore it tilted its head to the left. On hands and knees, Ginger crawled across the room and without touching the object, leaned down and squinted at it, hoping she'd been wrong the first time.

Nope. Still knocked up.

She rolled over onto her back, staring blindly at the ceiling. "How did this happen?" Okay, that time she didn't imagine the statue's head tilt. Right? "I mean, I know *how* this happens. I worked in a bar for seven years. You pick up a thing or two listening to people piss away their troubles over whiskey. But we were so damn careful."

A flush crept up her neck as a barrage of scenes starring her and Lieutenant Derek Tyler, her boyfriend of nearly a year, blurred together in her mind, starting the week she, Willa, and Dolly had moved in next door. They'd been on the lam, having fled Nashville to escape their dire circumstances. A cop had been her *last* choice in a neighbor. He'd wasted no time making his intentions clear. Very clear. She shook her head to dispel the visions of their naked, writhing bodies on various surfaces. "Don't look at me like that," she said to Dolly. "I remember that time at the Laundromat. And that weekend in Miami last month…"

Ginger slapped her palm to her forehead. Derek had surprised her with a last-minute trip to South Beach, having finally wrapped up a major case and deciding to take his very first vacation since joining the force. Never having been to Florida, let alone on a vacation, she'd forgotten her birth control pills in the excited rush to pack. At first, they'd been careful about using condoms, but there'd been that *one* single time. And wasn't that always the way it happened? That afternoon they'd spent on the beach, sipping mojitos. Swimming in the ocean, slipping against one another's wet bodies, tempting, heightening the anticipation. He'd growled over her choice of a purple string bikini, but she'd felt the effect it had on him. Hadn't wasted any opportunities to brush against him with her barely covered bottom, wrapping her legs around his waist, leaning over his impressively muscled chest to apply sunscreen.

By the time they stumbled, kissing and petting each other, into the hotel room, they'd been in a sexual frenzy. She'd been pulled down onto the floor, just inside their hotel room door. Her purple bikini had been torn from her body, baring her bottom to receive the mighty slap of Derek's palm…he'd been inside her before they remembered he hadn't worn a condom. By then, nothing short of a tsunami could have stopped them. Ginger remembered it clear as a bell, as if it had taken place five minutes ago instead of six weeks prior. There had been an illicitness to their lovemaking, as if the risk were adding a whole new element. Knowing they were gambling, in a sense, had made them twice as wild.

He'd finished with a roar, then flipped her over and taken her again. Harder.

Ginger cleared her throat in the silent room. "Well. I seem to have sorted out the *when* and I'll be keeping it to myself, Dolly, if you don't mind. Now on to the *why now*." She glanced over at the framed picture of her and Derek that sat on her bedside table. Derek kissing her forehead, arms wrapped around her protectively. Always protecting. So solid and reassuring. The picture had been taken by Willa, her photographer younger sister, when they were both unaware. It was the main reason she loved the picture. No posing or false smiles. Just the two of them as they were at that moment. Happy. At peace.

Would this unexpected news change that? Yes, they loved each other. Yes, this last year, without question, had been the happiest in her twenty-four years. But this…a baby…it would change everything. They'd never even discussed having children. Although to be fair, she suspected Derek would avoid that topic at the risk of sending her screaming for the hills. He knew every gory detail about her shitty upbringing, her issues surrounding family. Her mother had been a drug addict and a prostitute who'd turned tricks in their living room. Not exactly a shining example of motherhood in all its glory.

One of the insecurities she and Derek had set out to overcome was her intense fear of commitment. After watching her mother being used and discarded regularly, she'd never envisioned herself in a relationship. She'd only moved in with Derek a few months ago and while she loved him to an astonishing degree, it had been a monumental decision for her. The stubborn man had all but tricked her into it. A baby *epitomized* commitment. A lifetime's worth of it. She wasn't sure she was ready for that kind of thing. Even if she was…what about Derek?

She thought of herself nine months pregnant, wearing maternity clothes to accommodate her swollen belly. And allowed the tiny niggle of worry to creep in at the image. At age fourteen, she'd realized men liked the way she looked. Sure, she'd used it to her advantage. Even while luring Derek into what she'd thought would be a purely physical encounter. She didn't waste a moment regretting it, either. *Use what you've got* had been the words she'd lived by for so long. But since breaking free of her past and taking control of her life, she'd stopped relying on them. Her body's shape didn't define her anymore. Her self-confidence had grown exponentially since moving to Chicago and meeting Derek.

She was now a businesswoman. An actual role model to the sister she loved. Yet…she always knew the looks were at her disposal if she needed them. And perhaps a small, leftover part of her past self was worried that Derek wouldn't want her as much with cankles. She hated thinking that way. It was vain and silly. And yet.

"You understand, right, Dolly? You never leave the house

without your sequined bustier and blond wig." Okay, now *that* time the statue definitely shook its head disapprovingly. Pregnancy was apparently already taking its toll on her sanity. "Don't look at me like that. Everyone knows about the wigs and no one here is judging you. Especially the pregnant lady talking to a damn statue."

Raising a baby was simply not in her wheelhouse. While she may have grown emotionally and shed most of her hang-ups, it didn't mean she was ready for another human being to be completely dependent on her. She'd managed to raise Willa, now majoring in photography in college, through trial and error. Lord knew she'd made plenty of mistakes along the way. There'd been no time to prepare for this.

She doubted it was on Derek's radar, either. Not with his heavy workload, the way his peers relied on him. He'd been honored by the department earlier that year for his work in a sting operation involving two local gangs. She'd watched him accept his plaque from the Chicago police commissioner to thunderous applause from his colleagues, so choked with pride she could barely breathe. His career was on a major upswing. This would mean change. Sacrifices. Then, there was her own work. She'd opened Sneaky Peet's in Wicker Park, creating and selling custom furniture. Her designs had become so popular, her hours were nearly as demanding as Derek's. Throwing a baby into the equation at this stage, well, it was damned inconvenient.

Automatically, she felt an immense wave of guilt at her own thoughts. Slowly, very slowly, her hand crept to her still-flat belly and lay there. The world didn't end.

"Hell, Dolly. I'm screwed. I already love the little booger." She blew out a breath toward the ceiling. She would tell Derek. He would understand. He'd hold her and tell her everything was going to be all right. She had to believe in that. Believe in *him*. "Looks like the three of us are having a baby."

Chapter Two

Without looking up from his mountain of paperwork, Lieutenant Derek Tyler waved in the detective who'd just knocked tentatively on his glass office door.

"Do I not look busy enough to you, Alvarez?"

Most detectives knew when to back off around him. Not Alvarez, twenty-year veteran and all-around bullshit artist. He whistled softly through his teeth. "Someone's even testier than usual. I know you haven't been home to see your woman in two nights, but cut a dude some slack. Only doing my job."

Stone-faced, Derek simply let Alvarez squirm under his stare. He didn't like any of his men talking about Ginger. Not in any capacity. His woman. His business. Being that he'd spent the night away from their bed, instead of wrapped around her soft form where he belonged, he wasn't in the mood to make an exception for the ball-breaking detective. Derek had thought when she moved in with him, he wouldn't feel quite so anxious, unsettled, when he was forced to spend the night working. She'd be safe in his bed, behind a door he'd locked himself. Oddly, the desire to be home had grown exponentially. He should be home with her. Seeing to her needs. Demanding that she see to his. Spending every moment enjoying the fact that she'd taken that leap for him. With him.

His work-weary gaze strayed to the clock on his computer. Nine fifteen in the evening. She'd be spreading on lotion after a hot bath. Throwing on one of his department T-shirts. Nothing but tiny panties underneath. Sitting cross-legged on the floor cutting out pictures from magazines for her furniture designs, her brows drawn in concentration over her beautiful face. If he were to walk in the front door right now, she'd give him that hundred-watt smile and climb up his body for a long, wet, welcome-home kiss. God, as bad as he needed a fix of Ginger right now, he'd probably throw her down on the closest surface and fuck her hard and thorough before they'd even exchanged hellos.

So, no. He wasn't in the mood for this shit from Alvarez.

"The point. Get to it."

He threw up his hands. "Fair enough. Although by the time I'm finished giving you this report, you're going to wish you'd put it off a little longer."

"I highly doubt it."

"Don't say I didn't warn you." Alvarez flipped open the manila folder in his lap. "Two words. Gino Lazio."

Derek's spine stiffened, his entire body immediately on high alert. The paperwork on his desk suddenly became meaningless. His exhaustion a minor detail. Gino Lazio. Notorious crime boss on Chicago's South Side. Last year, a raid on the warehouse where Lazio's crew was making a major narcotics deal had ended in the loss of one of Derek's men. Lazio had been the one to pull the trigger. Then he'd disappeared without a trace. Derek's team had prevented the drug deal, temporarily disabled Lazio's crew, but there'd been no justice for the fallen officer—a fact that haunted him constantly. Relentlessly. He'd sat through the man's funeral, shook the hand of his crying widow...and he'd been unable to offer closure. Lazio had immediately gone to ground. They'd even heard through one informant that he'd been lying low in Italy, waiting for his chance to slip back into Chicago unnoticed. Not likely. Derek hadn't forgotten. Gino Lazio was his white whale.

"Tell me everything."

Alvarez had the good sense to keep a straight face. "As you know, we've had to pull our undercover officer embedded in the Lazio crew and relocate him. Things were getting too hot. They suspected a leak and he was new blood. Good news is, we've got an informant who continues to deliver. Lazio's nephew. We pick him up for cocaine possession like clockwork once a month and he spills his guts in exchange for leniency." Alvarez paused, seemingly for effect. "The kid swears Lazio is returning from Italy this week for a major meeting with Modesto's remaining crew."

Derek's eyes widened at that piece of news. He'd been commended by the department for leading the bust on the Modesto crew last year, right around the time he'd met Ginger. Trafficking charges had stuck to the major players, but a small portion of the crew had walked. "Lazio is absorbing the Modesto crew?"

Alvarez nodded once. "And their territory along with it."

"Can't let it happen." Derek meant every word. Lazio's operation, thanks to generations of experience dealing dirty in Chicago, was twice as sophisticated as Modesto's. If they were granted rights to more territory, the police would have a damned hard time containing it. They had ten times the men and enough firepower to cause serious damage to the city. His city. "When and where is this meet taking place?"

"That's the bitch of it. I leaned on the nephew for hours and he swore to every saint his junkie brain could remember that he doesn't know. He likes his freedom too much to bullshit me, Lieutenant."

Derek cursed under his breath. "Where the hell does that leave us?"

"Waiting on pins and fucking needles. That's where." Alvarez propped his booted foot on the edge of Derek's desk, removing it just as quickly when Derek scowled at him. "The kid says Lazio and company have grown too suspicious of the leak. The meeting time and place is going to be spur of the moment to avoid police interference. We have to be prepared to go at any time."

"I don't like it. We need more intel going into something this big."

"Working on it."

"Lazio and Modesto meeting," Derek mused. "Lazio sure as hell won't take any chances on getting caught. We've got an eyewitness in Detective Troy Bennett. That bullet killed his partner. He transferred to New York last year, but he'd fly back in a heartbeat to testify and put Lazio away."

Alvarez made a sound of agreement. "Yeah, he would. It's up to us to bring in Lazio, though. You were right about them not taking any chances. There's going to be more guns at this meeting than an NRA convention. Lazio is already a scary son of a bitch. Throw in the fact that he has nothing to lose? We're walking into a possible massacre."

Dread settled heavy in Derek's stomach. His eyes strayed to the picture of Ginger sitting on his desk. Blowing him a kiss in her purple bikini, the Miami sun setting in the background. Long, chestnut-colored hair in tumbling waves around her face. Brave, vulnerable, too-gorgeous-for-words Ginger. His reason for drawing breath.

Derek reminded himself that Alvarez was still waiting for a response. "You're right about that." He held his hand out for the folder and Alvarez handed it over. "But if we're successful, and I plan to make damn sure we are, this department will finally break the backs of both the Lazio and Modesto crews in one fell swoop."

Alvarez studied him for a moment. "All right. I'll leave you to plot the bad guys' respective downfalls, Lieutenant." The older man rose to exit the office, but paused with his hand on the doorknob. "You know what they call a raid like this?"

Derek arched an eyebrow.

"A widow-maker."

Long moments passed while Derek absorbed the implications of what he was taking on. The risks involved in taking down a dangerous crime family and their potential new partners. Was getting justice for one man and his family worth the risk? *Yes*, he thought without hesitation. How many men would they lose in the years to come if he allowed these criminals to remain loose on the streets? How many more widows? Fatherless children? This was his job. His responsibility. He had the power, the opportunity, to stop it. Turning a blind eye would be irresponsible. Beneath him.

Once again, his gaze landed on Ginger's smiling face in the photograph. She would protest mightily if she knew he considered her to be his responsibility as well. An infinitely more pleasurable one than his job, but a responsibility nonetheless. Hell, they were responsible to each other. She would lose her shit if she knew the danger he was getting ready to put himself in. Just like he'd lost *his* when she'd endangered herself last year in a stubborn attempt to do the right thing and return the $50,000 she'd stolen to create a new life for herself and Willa.

Derek raked a hand down his face. *Shit.* He couldn't tell her about the upcoming raid. Not without scaring the hell out of her. Their relationship thrived on honesty. He'd been the one to insist on that—to *demand* it, initially. Breaking through her barriers, earning her trust, hadn't been easy, but it had been the most rewarding accomplishment of his life.

He brushed his thumb over the photograph, imagining her beautiful face covered in tears. Her ability to love without the constant fear of *losing* that love was still fragile. The possibility of not holding her through the night, every single night for the rest of her life should things go bad, was a distraction he couldn't deal with right now. Distractions could cost lives—maybe his own.

He'd need to distance himself, he realized. The decision ate him alive, but it couldn't be helped. He had a responsibility to the fallen officer and needed to see it through.

Focus on the case. Plan it down to the smallest detail, take the fuckers down, and get back to your woman.

He brushed his thumb over the photograph again.

Try to understand, baby.

Chapter Three

Ginger rose from her kneeling position, intending to retrieve the furniture lacquer from under the sink, then froze. She frowned down at the decoupage nightstand she'd spent the afternoon decorating with magazine cutouts so they formed a cohesive collage. With the *9 to 5* soundtrack blasting from the stereo, she'd lost herself in the supposed Halloween design she'd been planning on displaying this week in her shop, leading up to the holiday.

Instead? Pink. Baby. Shit. Everywhere.

At this rate, she wouldn't need to drop the baby bombshell on Derek. He'd take one look at her latest creation and know she was *in the family way* within seconds. She wouldn't have the chance to prepare him carefully, like she'd planned. Or to stuff him full of her famous chicken potpie first. Her nervous gaze flew to the clock. Derek would be home any minute. With a muffled curse, she gripped the edge of the nightstand and dragged it into the nearest closet, slamming the door shut just as Derek entered the apartment.

Ginger took a moment to adjust her bra, tugging down

the snug material of her tank top while she was at it. No sense in letting a perfectly good cleavage day go to waste, right? If it made her feel slightly better going into the big reveal with a fully loaded arsenal, well, she wasn't harming a fly, was she?

She turned and cocked her hip, knowing her white cotton skirt would slide up her thigh with the action. Heaven help the man, he loved her thighs. "Hey, darlin'."

Loosening his tie, he watched her closely. "Ginger."

His deep voice traveled across the room to massage her senses. Fire licked in her belly, her loins, her breasts. He did it all to her with a single word. A year ago, when she'd moved in next door to Derek, this intense chemical reaction had alarmed her. Made her feel out of control. Needy. Powerless. Now, she knew better. She held just as much power as Derek. But Lord, did they wield that power in different ways.

Still observing her through heavy-lidded eyes across the room, he began rolling up his sleeves to reveal brawny forearms. Slowly. With intention. Her chest shuddered on a deep breath, pulse kicking up ten notches. Feet rooted to the floor, she could only watch and wait to determine his purpose. Not having seen him in nearly two days, she used the time to drink him in, appreciate the breathtaking man she shared a bed with. Derek managed to look at home in his suit, although she knew from experience he owned *whatever* he wore. Confident and sensual one minute. Challenging and ruthless the next. She'd once likened him to a barroom brawler, all cut muscles and harsh angles. A body she never got tired of tracing with her fingers, her tongue.

He regarded her steadily from behind green eyes, his demeanor casual. However, with his dark brown hair slightly mussed, she knew better. He had a habit of losing his patience with it when he wanted something. Usually her. The undercurrent of lust had already reached her, enfolding her to drag under its surface. It never took a day off. She couldn't escape the connection between them and didn't want to.

When he'd finished his appraisal, Derek rounded the couch and came toward her, each step purposeful. Already panting with need, Ginger let him walk her backward until her body made contact with the hard wall of the living room. His masculine scent, mixed with a hint of leather and coffee, caused her body to ready, recognizing its mate. She welcomed the warm, damp sensation between her thighs, knowing her readiness would please him. Derek braced his hands above her on the wall, but didn't make contact with her body. She wanted to sob a protest and pull him closer, but knew better than to push. Much as it pained her keeping quiet, patience always paid off with Derek.

He let his head drop down so he could speak, very precisely, near her ear. "Take my cock out."

This time she couldn't contain a whimper of anticipation. With shaky hands, Ginger quickly undid his belt buckle, movements slightly clumsy under his watchful gaze. His button and zipper came next. She could feel his weighty erection pressing against his boxer briefs. Unable to help herself, she took a moment to squeeze him, run her thumb up the sensitive underside.

"I didn't give you permission for that." His eyes were closed, a telling sign that despite his harsh words, her touch had certainly affected him. Then they snapped open, harder than before. "Reach inside, wrap me in your hand, and take me. The fuck. Out."

"Yes, Derek," she breathed, slipping her hand under the waistband of his briefs. "Since you asked so nicely." She tugged his underwear down his hips with the other. Before she could make contact with his thick arousal, Derek snagged her wrist, brought it to his mouth and licked her palm, provocative and slow, then released her. They both groaned into the silent apartment when she fisted his erection with her newly dampened hand. Whatever game he was playing, Ginger was a willing participant. The young woman she'd been when they met would have taken offense to being ordered around. This Ginger, *she* gloried in the part of her man that craved control. After all, at that moment, she held the concentration of that power right in her hand. Without her, his power didn't exist.

His hips began to thrust rhythmically, pushing his length into her grip. "Would you like to hear what happens next?"

She inhaled in a rush. "Yes, please. The devil is in the details."

"I guess that makes me the devil." One big, callused hand dropped to the outside of her thigh, coasting up her flesh just close enough to raise goose bumps on every inch of her body. Slipping underneath her skirt without hesitation. When he reached her backside, Ginger wanted to beg shamelessly for him to palm her roughly, knead her there. Instead, he merely brushed his fingers down the center of her bottom, along the cherry-red material of her thong. The simple touch had a devastating effect, every nerve ending singing with terrible, glorious need.

"I'm going to take some much-needed time with your mouth right now. While I do, you're going to continue stroking me until I'm so close to coming, I'll be ready to die just to drill you against this wall. But I won't. I'm going to stop you just before I bust. Then I'm going to lick the sweet pussy that's been waiting so patiently for me." He surged into her hand. "Come on, baby. Make me suffer."

Ginger's knees wobbled, lust pounding so insistently in her belly, she would climax from his words alone if he continued to speak. No. Derek would give her relief. Only Derek. She could feel it hovering already. Only if she followed his sensual instructions, though. Hell, she was eager to follow them. They'd been designed for her alone. Lifting her eyes to his, she massaged the crown of his erection with her thumb, reveling in his shortened breathing. When her fingers tightened and dipped to the base, rising in a firm, tight stroke, Derek's mouth swooped down with a growl to kiss her greedily. The kiss was far from gentle. It was raw, base agony translated through hot, slippery warmth. The sting of teeth. The smooth glides of their tongues. It consumed Ginger, scorching her where she stood. Unconsciously, her hand increased its pace to match the frenzied tempo of the kiss.

They broke apart, gasping for precious air at each other's lips. Her breath caught at the fierceness of his expression, but her hand didn't slow its ministrations. Subtly, she twisted her wrist on each stroke. Applied more pressure. Above her head, his fist punched the wall. "Just a little more. I'm almost there. Make it fucking hurt for me, beautiful girl."

"Let yourself go. Let me make you come, Derek. Please." Her plea escaped her without a thought. She didn't like seeing him in pain. Couldn't think past making it go away. He'd been away from her too long. Knowing him, he would refuse to lessen the urgent ache on his own.

"*No.*" His jaw flexed. The firm hand resting on her bare bottom squeezed her flesh, then slapped it, leaving a fresh sting in its wake. "You do what I tell you, Ginger. Or no tongue between your legs."

Oh God. She needed his mouth so badly. Her stomach muscles clenched tightly, moisture coating her core just imagining his dark head dipping between her thighs. She needed this torture to end. *Now.* Derek might refuse to take his release, but she wasn't nearly that proud. If she didn't find satisfaction soon, she might expire from the blistering need. "Yes, *Lieutenant.* I only do what you tell me," she whispered, knowing it would send him higher.

"Goddammit." He ripped her hand free. "You're lucky I'm dying for a fucking taste, or I would spank your ass raw for that."

"Lucky me," she whispered, shivering with anticipation.

With a sound of blatant hunger, Derek dropped to his knees before her. He curled his hands beneath her knees and draped them over his broad shoulders, effortlessly supporting Ginger's weight with his hands. Her panties were torn free. By his teeth? Hands? With her head lolling against the wall, eyes squeezed tightly shut, dying for that first lick, she couldn't care less about his method.

His pressed his mouth to her core. She felt the vibration of his moan as he nuzzled her, his stubble scraping the sensitive flesh of her inner thighs. Letting her weight rest on his shoulders, his hands were free to grasp her bottom, tilt her hips toward his mouth. "Soaked and slick, baby. Just how I like you."

"Oh, *please*. Give it to me." Too many sensations. Her nerve endings sizzled and snapped. The apartment blurred and tilted around them. "*Derek*. I can't…"

She heard his dark laughter, then ceased to think altogether.

...

Derek sampled his woman with teasing licks, purposefully avoiding the tender spot dying for his attention. Fuck, she tasted like…Derek abandoned every adjective his lust-fogged brain could manage, discarding them as inadequate. She tasted like *his*. That's what the fuck she tasted like. When she screamed *yes, yours* above him, Derek realized he'd repeated his internal sentiment out loud. Good. She needed to be told regularly who she belonged to.

He continued to lap at her until her thighs squeezed his head. Until her whimpered words stopped making sense. Then, only then, did he relent, gently stabbing her clitoris with his tongue until she screamed, only to lick it soothingly, murmuring his praise, apologies, filthy words against her damp flesh.

He spread her thighs as far as they would go and fit his mouth snugly over her clit, sucking, rolling it on his tongue. Her hips writhed and bucked, trying to get closer, and he knew she was seconds away from her peak. Nails dug into his shoulders, his hair, as if not knowing where to settle. Her disjointed motions undid him. He'd driven her out of control of her own body. It exhilarated him every time. After one final, sweet suck, Derek pulled back slightly and circled his tongue over her spot once, twice, and felt her begin to shake. Desperate to taste the pleasure he'd wrought, he slid his tongue past her opening, groaning at the feel of her tightening on him.

"Oh God. Derek. Oh *God*."

Her taste was like an aphrodisiac to his system. The pulsing ache between his legs grew too fierce. His body demanded he seek release. Surge up between her legs and claim her. Fuck her like an animal against the wall. But he couldn't do it. Even in this state of blind need, his conscience weighed down on him. His decision to keep her in the dark about his case was the gritty layer of deceit stopping him. There hadn't been a single barrier between them in a long time and he resented it. Resented himself. So he wouldn't allow himself the complete comfort of her body. Through his lie of omission, he was withholding a part of himself. Something he'd promised never to do again.

Tense with self-disgust, Derek wrapped a fist around his erection. Using Ginger's perfect taste to drown out every other thought, he climaxed into his own hand, growling against her core as the spasms racked his body.

When the tremors subsided in both of them, Derek lay his face on her taut belly, listened to her breathing turn even after a few minutes. He wanted to stay just like that forever, but knew it was impossible. Already he could sense her confusion, possibly even hurt, over the unusual end to their lovemaking. He always found release inside of her. Always. Nothing he'd encountered in this world compared to it. Now, because he hadn't, she obviously sensed something was wrong.

"Derek? Did something happen at work?" Her fingers slid hesitantly into his hair, sending tingling warmth down his spine. "I'm right here. T-talk to me."

Hating the note of uncertainty in her voice, he pulled her down onto his lap. She tucked herself against him immediately, trusting, comforting. It made him feel like the biggest bastard alive even as his heart swelled with love.

"Everything is fine, baby." He started to stroke her hair, but curled his fist against the urge. "I just had a long day."

Ginger nodded, her head bumping his chin. Tenderness shot through him, battling the guilt momentarily. Then she opened her mouth and obliterated that sliver of progress. "Derek, you know how we talked about the importance of us being honest with each other? Tell each other everything, no matter how big or small?"

Steel banded his throat, choking off his air so all he could do was grunt.

"So…if there were something sort of big that might change things…you would still want me to tell you. Right?"

Christ, this had to be the worst kind of punishment. She wanted to open up, communicate something important to him. Progress for headstrong, independent Ginger on so many levels. However, if he listened to it, witnessed her honesty, he would either feel obligated to reciprocate, or continue to keep his silence. Either way, he would feel like a son of a bitch. His options were scare her or lie to her. He found both of them equally unappealing.

At that moment, with the center of his universe wrapped around him on the floor of their home, Derek felt secure enough to admit something else to himself. He felt...*fear* over the upcoming raid. Fear of failing. The possibility of losing more men. Dying himself and leaving Ginger alone. So many things. Prior to meeting Ginger, he'd never experienced a real moment of fear in his life. It had simply never been part of his emotional makeup. Then a year ago, Ginger had put her life at risk and he'd been forced to race the clock in order to save her.

He remembered that first sharp sting of fear so clearly, it still gave him vivid nightmares. He had something to lose now. Having something of value in his life meant getting used to feeling fear, but it would take time. Now? It still felt too fresh. If he were to come clean to Ginger about the danger ahead, he would see his own fear reflected in her face. It would stay with him when the inevitable moment came to risk his life. He'd never be able to perform his duty, knowing what it would do to her if he never came home. Just like the fallen officer whose death he needed to avenge. The thought of leaving Ginger, when he'd promised so many times he never would, battered his heart. His only choice was to stay silent. Make damn sure that by the time she learned of the case, he was already on his way home to her.

Praying he would find the words to explain his reasoning to her someday, Derek took a deep breath. Then did one of the hardest things he'd ever done in his life. Without answering her earnest, endearing questions, he eased Ginger off his lap and pulled them to their feet. "I just remembered I left some work unfinished at the station. Can it wait until later?"

Hurt clouded her features for a split second before she hid it. He *hated* that she hid it, even though the blame sat squarely on his shoulders. She closed into herself then, in a way that would be imperceptible to anyone but himself.

The man who knew her inside and out. With a chuckle, she straightened her clothing and marched into the kitchen, spine so rigid, he feared she might crack. "At least take a potpie with you. No reason to starve while you're out saving the whole damn world, Lieutenant." Her movements briskly efficient, she drew a pie out of the oven and snapped it into some Tupperware. When she handed it to him, she didn't quite meet his eyes.

"Ginger..."

"What is it?" she burst out. "You got exactly what you came home for. What else is there to say?"

A voice shouted in his head, ordering him to pull her into his arms. Demand she hand over her burden, even though he couldn't make a fair trade with his own. He wanted to reassure her, but couldn't. The longer the silence stretched, the easier it was to read disappointment in her eyes. She'd never looked at him that way before and it slayed him.

"Go to work, Derek."

He watched her turn and shut herself into the bedroom before he left, loathing every step that took him farther away from her. All the while knowing it didn't even compare to the distance he'd just created.

Chapter Four

Ginger accepted cash from the customer and handed him his receipt. "Is the chest a gift for your wife or did you just make her mad?"

He laughed as he tucked the slip of paper into his leather wallet. "It's a gift. Although I make her mad often enough that I'll definitely be back."

"Good." She winked at him. "I'll set aside the matching bureau."

"Consider it a sale." His eyes twinkled. "For when she finds out I bought those Cubs season tickets."

Her smile was a little wistful as she watched the older gentleman, with the help of his eager-to-please son-in-law, carry out the French two-drawer chest. She always felt this way watching one of her favorite pieces walk out the door, but it bolstered her mood knowing it was going to a good home. Not to mention the hefty price tag.

Two young mothers walked into the store chatting animatedly, their respective children entering behind them like hurricanes hell-bent on destroying her shop. Both dressed as Captain America, they skidded to a stop in front of the cash register and held out their pillowcases to her, toothy smiles a mile wide.

"Trick or treat!"

Ginger shared a laugh with the mothers as she reached under the counter to retrieve her bowl of mini Snickers bars. Wicker Park, the neighborhood in which she'd chosen to open her store, was full of young families, unique shops, and experimental restaurants. She loved it here. The unique, funky sensibility of the locals layered over a strong foundation of family. The more she witnessed those unbreakable bonds of mother-child, husband-wife, even pet-to-owner, the more she understood it. Somewhere along the line, the foreign concept of unconditional love had started making sense to her. It hadn't seemed so impossible anymore. Maybe, just maybe, she could have that for herself. With Derek.

How that careful building of confidence and hope could shatter so quickly, she didn't honestly know. Five nights ago, waiting for Derek to come home, she'd been so damn sure of his reaction to the news that she was pregnant. The entire day, she'd become more and more convinced that a new life could be a good thing. An amazing thing. She'd tell him she was carrying their baby. He would pull her close and share in her joy.

Never, not once, in the thousand scenarios she'd created in her head, did Derek walk away before she could share the news. He'd never actually *been* there to begin with, she'd realized afterward. Sitting in the bedroom, hearing the front door close, she'd replayed the scene in her head. Derek coming home, giving her an unbelievable sexual experience, yet withholding that final part of himself. Pleasuring himself without the use of her body. He'd been distant. Something had been missing. But she'd still kept her faith, her *hard-won* faith, because this was Derek. And he loved her.

Then he'd shut her down. She could still feel that cold, empty feeling. A feeling she'd never expected to associate with her lover. Her best friend. Her everything.

"Two Captain Americas?" Ginger forced a smile. "Are you planning on catching lots of bad guys tonight? You boys have certainly got your work cut out for you. I've seen quite a few questionable characters lurking around outside my shop."

"We'll get them for you!" One boy raised his shield proudly into the air. When the other boy tried to imitate his friend, his shield clattered to the ground. They both tried to pick it up and bumped heads. Ginger wanted to laugh with the mothers, but instead she felt suspiciously like crying.

Quickly, she shoveled a handful of Snickers into each bag. "I feel much safer now. Now, you listen to your mamas. Don't eat too much candy or you won't be able to fly."

"We won't. Thank you!"

Seconds later, they'd run out of the store, already moving on to their next candy conquest. Trying to distract herself, she rearranged the furniture to account for the hole left by the just-bought piece. Time had moved at an odd pace that week. Slow at times and fast at others. She still couldn't manage to wrap her mind around the fact that Derek hadn't come home in five whole days. Sure, he'd called and texted, but his tone had been stiff, businesslike. He'd clearly been rushing to get off the phone. Since the day he'd walked out, she'd existed in a kind of dreamlike state, every day flowing into the next. The longer she went without seeing him, the more she was convinced something was wrong between them. She just had no idea what it could be.

Tonight, she and Derek were supposed to attend a Halloween party at an ex-police dispatcher's house. Patti, a grandmotherly-type, had been Derek's right-hand lady during her days working at the station. She'd retired earlier this year, but still made it a point to issue them invites to her many themed get-togethers. They *always* had a theme. Hawaiian night. Brad Pitt night. Speakeasy night. Patti was a beloved member of the department, so officers and their wives, new recruits all the way up to senior law enforcement, showed up. Even Ginger, who'd seen her fair share of parties, had to admit they were a good time.

Thankfully her costume for tonight didn't have to revolve around a specific theme. She'd picked up a gypsy costume from the seasonal costume shop down the block during her lunch break. Since she'd waited until the very last minute, her choices had boiled down to gypsy and nun. Which, in Ginger's thinking, hadn't really been a choice at all. Besides, sheer crop tops and low-riding skirts would be off-limits once her belly started to grow.

Might as well get her kicks before the baby started to kick.

Derek would normally hate the costume on sight, but she didn't know what to expect when she saw him tonight. Perhaps he'd be back to his normal self, his odd behavior a mere blip on the radar caused by too many hours at work. God, she hoped it was the case.

Her cell phone buzzed on her desk, signaling an incoming text message. Before Ginger even glanced at the screen, she knew. Deep down, she knew what it would say.

Can't make it tonight. Have fun. Be safe. Derek.

Slowly, she replaced the phone on the counter. Could she actually be losing him? Had she been so caught up in her newfound happiness that she'd missed some invisible warning sign? Was fate playing a cruel joke on her? Derek couldn't be pulling away now. Not when she was carrying his child. For the first time in a long time, she felt…alone. So alone. Abandoned.

That old fear, the long-buried insecurity about becoming

her mother, snuck up on her. It threatened to drag her down into its churning depths, but she determinedly scared it back into its cage. Nothing, not even the soul-shattering possibility of losing Derek, could turn her into that. Into a mother who left her children to fend for themselves for weeks on end while she played house with her latest boyfriend. Drinking, getting high. Until she'd fulfilled her worth and he kicked her out. No. Ginger had already accepted responsibility for the baby in her belly and she would be the best goddamn mother her limited knowledge allowed.

A group of laughing kids running past the shop brought her back to the present. Moving on shaky legs, she locked the store's entrance and turned the sign to *closed*. She went to the back office, threw herself down into the leather swivel chair, and stared at the risqué gypsy costume hanging on the back door. Briefly, she wondered if she could return it and get her money back. Then she thought, *what the hell for?* So Derek had decided to skip the party. Didn't mean she had to, right?

Ginger welcomed the blast of her familiar spirit, could practically feel her tough exterior moving into place over her skin, locking together. Armoring her against the ability to feel anything. She'd worked long and hard to drop that armor, but right now, it felt smooth as a second skin. So Derek had written her off? He'd rather work than spend time with her or listen to what she had to say? Fine with her. She wasn't dead. She'd go to the party, drink nonalcoholic beverages, and have a grand time without his big, bossy ass.

She shot to her feet and snagged the costume off the door.

• • •

Derek sat across the street, parked in his black SUV, waiting for Ginger to walk out of Sneaky Peet's. He'd taken a longer route than necessary on his drive back from a meeting with the commissioner, hoping to catch a glimpse of her. She usually left at six, but tonight she'd worked late. It was now well past eight. More often than not, he would be waiting for her at the curb to take her home. Not today. If he spent five minutes in her presence and saw a hint of uncertainty or doubt on her face, he'd spill everything. They'd received information that the raid would go down tonight. He'd anticipated the news, already having predicted the meeting would go down on Halloween, when the police department was distracted elsewhere. Just one more night and he could put the case behind him. Firmly in his past where it wouldn't continue to haunt him. One more night and he could hold her again, knowing he was giving her, giving *them*, everything.

Damn, he missed her. It had been five miserable days, and he felt hollow without her. Such a short period of time, yet for them, five days felt like a lifetime. He missed the way she perched on the bathroom sink while he shaved and talked about her plans for the day. He missed the way she put her hands on her hips when she cooked, muttering under her breath that she had to be missing something. He missed waking up with her sweet-smelling hair in his face. Her feet tucked between his legs.

He'd forgone all those privileges by sleeping, showering, eating at the station. Practically working around the clock with hour-long naps when he could take them. He couldn't go home and look her in the eye. See the confusion, the hurt on her face.

She hadn't responded to his earlier text. While Derek honestly hadn't expected one, he hadn't seen her moving around in the store for long minutes. Had she already left and he'd missed her? Not a chance in hell. *Maybe I'll just go check.* He wouldn't be able to concentrate on anything until he saw her now. Derek placed his hand on the door handle, intending to exit the car, just as Ginger left the shop.

"*Fucking Christ.*"

Derek's mouth went dry at the sight of her. The rest of his body reacted just as swiftly, every inch of him tensing. Preparing. His cock felt ready to burst from behind his fly, the swiftness of it causing his vision to blur. And that was before she even turned around.

Her purple velvet skirt flared out from her hips, over her pert little ass. Then it ended. *No.* It was too short. Her thighs were too exposed. If she bent over...fuck. He couldn't think about her bending over. He'd need immediate fulfillment and she was out of his reach right now. His growl of frustration echoed in the car's interior.

Ginger finished locking the door of the shop and turned in his direction, seemingly unaware of the reaction she'd just caused. His attention became arrested on her face. Her full, red lips, darkly made-up eyes. She looked exotic. Ripe. Sensual. Even more gorgeous than usual. Hand gripping the steering wheel so hard the leather groaned under the pressure, Derek's gaze dropped helplessly to her breasts. Pressing snugly against the white ruffle serving as a goddamn shirt, they looked fucking delectable. He wanted her straddling him at that moment in the car so he could suck her nipples until she peaked. He wouldn't allow her to remove the top either. He would suck her right through that sorry excuse for clothing.

A yellow cab pulled to a stop at the curb and Derek shook his head, even knowing she couldn't see him. She wasn't going anywhere dressed like that. Not without him. After casting an absent glance to determine there was no oncoming traffic, he flung the car door open.

"*Ginger.*"

She jerked to a stop in the act of climbing into the cab, eyes wide in surprise as they landed on him forty yards away. Based on her visible reaction, Derek had an idea of the look on his face. Fucking pissed. Possibly a little deranged. A whole lot of aroused. He couldn't care less. His objective was to stop her from getting into the cab. Going somewhere and being around other men who would look at his woman.

"Come over here," he called, his voice deep and purposeful.

For a minute, she simply stared. Then her chin went up. "No."

The challenge burned in his gut and frankly, turned him on even more. "No?"

She tossed her purse into the backseat and sent him a wink. "Have a good night, darlin'. Don't work too hard."

"I swear to God, Ginger—"

"Oh, you do? Well, as long as you're chatting with God, can you ask him what happened to my boyfriend?" When words failed him, she shrugged, hazel eyes shining. "Because I'm damn tired of wondering."

Her words pelted him like stones, but Derek wasn't giving up the fight. He waited for a car to pass, then stalked toward her, intending to bodily place her in his passenger seat, drive her home, and fuck her silly in their bed. It couldn't be helped any longer. His need was a drumming, aching pain. Ginger was the only one who could cure him.

He could cure her, too. He could fix this. It wasn't just about sex anymore for him, although he wouldn't deny the insane need thickening with each passing moment.

Something in her expression, her rigid demeanor, alarmed him. What he'd done, the manner in which he'd left that day, had somehow set them back. So much further than he'd originally thought. She didn't just appear confused. There was fear and *finality* there. It pummeled him. What the fuck?

She moved too fast, ducking into the cab, slamming the door, and signaling the driver to go. With a growled curse, he sprinted back to his SUV and followed.

Chapter Five

Letting the cool October breeze wash over her through the open taxi window, Ginger watched the familiar residential neighborhood pass by in a blur. Costumed children raced up and down the sidewalks, their exasperated parents attempting to keep up, reminding them to say *please* and *thank you*. Bare trees and dead leaves decorating the ground called to mind her first month in Chicago late last fall. She remembered the fear of striking out on her own. Wondering if she was doing the right thing. Somehow, she'd circled back to the beginning, but couldn't remember taking a wrong turn.

    A memory rose unbidden to her mind, blindsiding Ginger in her current state. Derek surprising her on a Friday afternoon last spring, showing up at Sneaky Peet's to take her to lunch. They'd driven to the Lincoln Park Lagoon, sat in the grass, and watched students paddle by in kayaks. Talked about their mornings. She'd laid her head in his lap and drifted off to sleep in her newfound happiness while Derek stroked her hair. Not knowing how long she'd been asleep, she'd woken with a start to find Derek watching her. His expression had stolen her breath. Derek didn't express himself the way most men did. He didn't use flowery language or buy the typical gifts men bought women. That day by the lagoon, however, she'd caught him off guard. His expression had been such a stunning mix of tenderness and awe, she'd been unable to do anything but stare back.

He'd brushed his thumb over her bottom lip, throat working with emotion. "Sometimes I look at you...and I can't breathe around these feelings." She'd started to speak, but he put his hand over her mouth. A move that, coming from Derek, wasn't meant to be offensive. It only meant he wasn't finished. "If you ever want anything in this world, promise me right now you'll tell me what it is. I want the honor of killing myself to make it happen. Promise."

She'd nodded vigorously and the second he removed his hand, she'd thrown herself into his arms. Neither one of them had returned to work that day. They simply couldn't bring themselves to separate.

Valiantly, Ginger tried to stop thinking about Derek, about the sweet memory and the ugly scene outside her shop moments ago. Instead, she focused on regaining the attitude she'd had in her office. She wouldn't *allow* herself to feel anything. Her other option was to curl up in a ball of self-doubt and anxiety over what the future held. She refused to be that person. So, for tonight, she'd be the girl who hid everything behind her smile. Again.

The cab pulled to a stop in front of Patti's home, a three-story clapboard house painted bright robin's-egg blue. Judging from the crowd spilling out onto the front lawn, the party was in full swing. Immediately, Ginger spotted a few of Derek's detectives on the porch. Noticing they weren't wearing costumes, but their uniforms instead, she frowned. They looked tense. None of them were holding drinks.

The cab driver cleared his throat, demanding her

attention. She handed him her fare through the partition and exited onto the sidewalk.

Several people called out greetings to her as she walked up the path to Patti's house. People she genuinely liked whom she'd met at similar parties, or Derek's work functions over the past year. She gave them her biggest, bravest smile, waving at them as she passed. Behind her, she heard a vehicle screech to a stop at the curb. Without turning around, she knew it was Derek. An unconscious part of her had known he would follow. Whether or not he'd decided to move on from their relationship, he still desired her physically. Would still consider her *his* until he'd stated otherwise. A man like Derek didn't relinquish control so easily. Half of her hated him for it. The other half was thankful he'd come. It confirmed he still felt something for her.

Pretending to be oblivious to his presence, she increased her pace slightly, hoping to escape into the house before he reached her. Perhaps she was running from the inevitable confrontation, but decided to cut herself from slack. Walking into a party, feeling as though she could fly apart at any moment, was enough pressure to face for now. Derek called her name, but the loud music pumping from the house gave her a valid reason to ignore him. As if she hadn't heard.

Ginger spotted Patti the moment she walked into the house and wound her way through several groups of people complimenting one another on their costumes. Again, she noticed many officers were wearing their uniforms. Looking tense, they huddled together and talked amongst themselves. Even Detective Alvarez, whom she now considered a dear friend, only managed a quick nod in her direction before returning to his discussion. The rest of the party guests seemed oblivious to the serious officers, however, dancing and drinking as though they didn't have a care in the world.

She placed a hand on Patti's arm and the woman turned

to her with such a warm, welcoming smile, Ginger felt thankful she'd come. No matter what happened, these were still her friends. Her surrogate family. She even laughed when she realized Patti had dressed up as Olive Oyl. To her left stood her long-suffering husband in a Popeye getup.

"Ginger!" Patti exclaimed. "You came! And look at you dressed to kill. If I had a body like that, I swear on this martini, I'd walk around naked. You wouldn't get me in pants. Not even for church."

Ginger laughed, painfully aware that Derek was only seconds behind her. She could only hope he'd been waylaid by some of his detectives. "You know you look good, Patti. I say give those church folks an eyeful. Give them something to talk about."

"Don't encourage her," Patti's husband chimed in drily before tossing back his drink.

Patti rolled her eyes, but Ginger could see the affection between them. It produced another pang in her chest. A look of sympathy crossed Patti's features. "I'm actually surprised you came. With everything going on, that is."

Ginger quirked an eyebrow. "What's...going on?"

The older woman cleared her throat, suddenly appearing uncomfortable. Ginger felt her heart sink to her stomach. Did Patti know something she didn't? Did she just inadvertently confirm what Ginger had already suspected about Derek wanting to end things? She remembered the uncomfortable demeanor of the officers when she'd arrived. Their quiet discussion. Did everyone know? Were they pitying her? Ginger took a shaky step backward and bumped into a hard chest. Derek's hands banded around her arms.

His words landed on her like a falling piano. "We need to talk."

Patti split a nervous glance between them, then ducked her head. Ginger realized then, beyond a shadow of a doubt, she'd been right. Her instincts had told her this was coming. Even now, Patti couldn't meet her eyes. Derek finally wanted to talk. Which had to mean she was moments away from the worst emotional pain in her life. No, this couldn't be happening. Not after everything. Not after her finally learning how to trust. Jesus, had he already moved on to someone else? Was her replacement here at the party?

So easily he could cast her aside. Just like all those men in her mother's life, with their lies and false promises. She'd fallen for it hook, line, and sinker. Dammit, she thought she'd been so careful to avoid the trap. The trap of becoming anything even remotely resembling her mother.

Ginger felt exposed. Vulnerable. And after a moment, pissed as hell. She'd told him this would happen. That trust was for suckers and happiness didn't last. At the end of the day, you could trust only yourself. She remembered all those nights he'd spent away over the last week and felt sick to her stomach. Hated herself for lying in their bed, wearing his T-shirt. So trusting. So stupid.

No way in hell would she give him the satisfaction of breaking her. If she was getting dumped the same week she found out she was pregnant, so what? Worse things had happened to her and she'd come through them stronger. This wouldn't kill her. It might come damn close, but she would fight through. And she'd be damned if she gave him the satisfaction of seeing her brought low.

With a toss of her hair, she pushed away from him. "I don't feel like talking. I feel like dancing." With that, she clicked out of the kitchen on her heels. It felt good, voluntarily walking away from him, putting that signature swagger in her step. *Eat your heart out, dickhead.*

Lithely, she snaked through the crowd to the living room at the back of the house. Furniture had been removed to give the guests room to dance. A dozen couples were moving to the popular music, plastered against each other. This is where the younger guests had congregated, Ginger noted. Away from the agitated police officers and prying eyes. Good. She was young, too, wasn't she? Sure, she was months from being a mother—a duty she would perform to the best of her ability. For the moment, though, she needed to think about something else. She needed to *feel* something. Anything to delay the inevitable.

Ginger tossed her purse onto a nearby table, careful to avoid knocking over any of the other dancers' drinks. She turned toward Derek, who'd followed her through the crowd, an unreadable expression on his chiseled face. When those eyes tracked down her body, she felt a powerful surge of arousal. He still wanted her. She could have him *right now*. She could be the one to walk away afterward. It would give her something to take with her. Grant her some goddamn pride.

She let her fingers track slowly up her bare thighs, swaying gently to the music. A few interested glances were thrown in her direction, but for the most part, people were concentrated on their own dance partner. Good. She was just getting started.

Derek rubbed a hand over his mouth. "Ginger."

Crooking a finger at him, she dipped her hips in time with the music. "Come here, Lieutenant."

"Stop this now." He took a step forward, spoke near her ear so she could hear him over the music. "I didn't want to do this here…"

Desperation bloomed in Ginger's chest. Oh God, he was going to break her heart right here and now? She'd had no time to prepare, even though she knew no amount of preparation would soften the blow. But…maybe she could delay it. She wanted, *needed*, to hinder the ax's descent at all costs. *Not yet. Not yet.* She moved closer, molded her body to his. Feeling his rigid arousal boosted her confidence. Ginger twined her arms around his neck, circled her hips against his, heard him groan. She closed her eyes and let their time together blur into a series of erotic images. Allowed herself to want him. As if she ever had a choice in the first place. Since he was challenging her own, she tapped into his pride, knowing it would have a devastating effect on him. He would never be able to resist it. And she meant every word.

"Derek. I was so lonely this week without you." She dragged her fingernails down his chest, opened her mouth on his throat. "You left me unsatisfied in our bed. I needed you, but you didn't come to me. I ached. And you weren't there."

His chest rumbled with a near-violent growl. "Stop it."

She turned methodically, undulating as she danced. Her bottom brushed strategically against his arousal and his fingers dug into the flesh of her hips. To prevent her or encourage her, she couldn't tell. Ginger was starting to wonder who was seducing whom when a sharp, blistering tug in her belly nearly buckled her knees. It had been too long. Her body was needy for his.

No. Attempting to retain focus, she shook herself. Tried to fight through the need. She pushed a button she knew would send him past his breaking point. "I wore this costume for a reason. I knew you'd hate it. Knew you'd *show* me how much you hate it."

Another deep groan. "Did you want to feel my displeasure?" Derek's fingers brushed down her naked stomach, inched slightly lower. Ginger was grateful for the near-darkness. She knew her face was flushed, her nipples pouting from their need to be touched.

"Yes. I want to feel your displeasure *now*."

His hand circled her wrist, unrelenting as steel. Before she could judge his intention, he pulled her from the living room and down a hallway, his stride sure and purposeful. He led her into a dim room. A home office, Ginger registered absently, then she could think no more. Derek whirled her around and his mouth came down on hers. His lips, tongue, and breath were familiar counterpoints to her own that had become vital to her survival. She immediately went under a tidal wave of hot, unrelenting desire. Even with uncertainty swirling around them, his touch grounded her immediately. She resented it even as she let it consume her. Drag her into its depths.

She sucked in a breath when his hands gripped her bottom and hitched her high on his body. Craving contact with him, Ginger locked her legs at the small of his back, crying out when he set her down on a low file cabinet and ground himself against her in a rough, urgent move. Her thin panties were almost nonexistent as they encountered the stiff material of his uniform pants, molded around his erection.

"How hard do you want to be fucked?"

Letting her thighs fall open, she whimpered. "No holding back this time. I don't want your mouth or your fingers. Not like last time. Give me what I deserve."

His green eyes lit with a dangerous fire. Ginger knew she'd found his limit. Not only had she told him he'd left her unfulfilled in their bed in his absence, she'd implied their last encounter hadn't satisfied her. It wasn't the truth, not remotely, but he reacted in the way she wanted. Needed. In one swift movement, he yanked her off the cabinet, whirled her around and bent her over. Her panties turned to rags in his hand as he rent them from her body. She threw her head back in reckless anticipation as his palm came down *hard* on her ass in a serious of stinging blows. Each time his hand connected with her backside, a groan issued from his throat, driving her wild in the knowledge that his need matched her own.

"Enjoy it, baby. You fucking begged for it, didn't you? Do

you enjoy wielding your power over me? You like turning me into an animal? Crazed to fuck?"

"*Yes*," she moaned.

"Good. Except now it's my turn." *Slap. Slap.* "And you've put me in a bad motherfucking mood, Ginger. I'm not going to stop pounding until the shape of my cock permanently exists inside of you. Until you can't move an inch without feeling me. Now, say my goddamn name."

He thrust into her with such force, Ginger screamed his name at the top of her lungs. Thankfully, the music drowned out her cries, because they didn't cease. Derek drove into her, relentless in his assault. Beneath her, the file cabinet scraped along the ground, propelling them forward until it wedged securely against the wall. Shameless, desperate, she spread her legs, lifted her ass. Her forehead connected with the wall and pressed into its dense surface, eyes squeezed tightly shut as the exquisite pressure built.

"Did you miss me?" He drove deep and held until she writhed and moaned. "You're *supposed* to miss me. You're supposed to *crave* me. If I'm not the last goddamn thought in your head before you fall asleep, I haven't been fucking you good enough." He brought his hand down in a loud smack of her right buttock. "And I think we both know that's not the case, don't we?"

When she didn't answer, he repeated the question more harshly. "Yes!"

"Yes, what?"

"It's…you…"

"I satisfy you every fucking time."

"Yes. *Yes*."

"And so do you." Derek braced himself on the wall above them and changed the pace of his thrusts. Deepening them. Prolonging them. "You think I haven't been miserable at the idea of you alone in our bed? Soft, warm, and tight? I've been crazed, baby. I can't concentrate. I've been starved."

"Then *why*?" Orgasm looming so close, the words tore from her throat. She couldn't think past the onslaught of sensation, even though his words didn't make sense. This was the end, right? Yes. It was. *Savor it. It'll never be this way again.*

"Ginger. *Ginger.*" Her name became a chant on his lips, matching the forward drives of his hips. The file cabinet slammed against the wall with each rough push. She absorbed his need, let it mesh with her own until the force of it buried her in an avalanche of fire and ice, radiant pleasure, a maelstrom of mixed emotions. Knowing it could be the last of its kind, she let the climax flay her, leave her revealed as she collapsed onto the metal cabinet, hearing Derek growl his release before he followed.

His heart pounded against her back, a feeling she used to adore, but now every beat sent pain lancing through her chest. When his lips moved in her hair, nuzzling, laying soft kisses, she pushed herself off the cabinet purely in the name of self-preservation. Ginger couldn't take a second more. She was horrified to find tears clouding her vision as she backed away from him. They were accompanied by a buzzing in her head. Disgusted with herself, her inability to maintain her composure long enough to accept the inevitable, she dragged in a shuddering breath. When he came toward her, worry and confusion in his eyes, it only made her more determined.

"Goddamn you, Derek." Fingers shaking, she pulled her panties back into place and smoothed her skirt. Just for the sake of something to occupy her vision. Looking at him hurt too much. "Do it. Say the words and get it over with."

She sensed Derek go very still. "Do what, exactly? Explain yourself. Now."

At the soft, dangerous quality to his voice, Ginger's gaze snapped to his. "You know." She whispered the words, finally unable to stop the flow of tears.

Loud voices shouted Derek's name in the hallway. Neither of them moved, but very slowly, his eyes closed and he cursed under his breath as if he'd been expecting the interruption. In a few quick, efficient movements, he repaired his state of undress. He took Ginger by the wrist and pulled her behind him as he opened the door.

"Lieutenant. There you are." Alvarez. "Let's roll. We've got a time and location. I've made the calls, but we've got to move. Less than an hour to go."

"I need a minute." His voice was deadly quiet.

"Boss, Lazio isn't going to wait—"

"A *minute*."

Lazio. Ginger's spine straightened, mind racing. She knew the name well. The case Derek had such a difficult time discussing, even with her. He'd lost a man, taken it hard. Of course he had. That was Derek. A leader. A protector. What was happening involving Lazio? In the living room, she heard a commotion, men talking in codes into their police radios. Everything she'd experienced during the week, everything she'd seen since walking into the party, suddenly took on a completely different quality. Tension among the officers, Derek working long hours. Something big was about to go down. Her terror outweighed her earlier pain so extremely then, it nearly doubled her over.

"Derek, what's going on?"

Leaving the door open a crack, he turned to her, strain showing on his face. He studied her intensely. "When you told me to get it over with, what were you talking about?"

The words felt like they might choke her. "I-I thought…" God, was it possible she could have been so wrong? Doubted him so easily? "You stopped coming home, you wouldn't talk to me…I thought it was over. I thought you wanted this over."

More shouts of his name in the hallway. He ignored them.

"Over," he repeated woodenly, the word sounding foreign coming from his lips.

His obvious shock confirmed it. Oh God. She hadn't trusted him enough. Now he was leaving, heading into a risky situation, her lack of faith fresh in his mind. "I'm sorry," she said numbly, knowing her words were inadequate.

Derek's hands rose to frame her face, holding it tightly. "How can you not know by now? I wouldn't make it a fucking day without you." He shook his head. "I don't remember a time before you. It's all a blur right up until the minute you walked in."

His face swam in front of her, her love for him so painfully intense it almost buckled her. Relief was short-lived, however, compared to the fear now permeating her nervous system. The shouts in the hallway were increasing. Time was running out and she still didn't know what Derek was heading into. How could he expect her to let him walk away right now? Jesus, he still didn't even know she was carrying his baby. *No.* She couldn't let him go. "Derek. Remember when you told me you'd give me anything in the world? Anything. You said I only had to ask."

"Yes." He brushed her tears away gently, as if he already knew what she was going to request. "And I'll do it. If you ask me, I'll stay right here." Their lips met briefly. "But this is something I have to do, so I'm asking you not to do that."

She dropped her head forward to rest on his chest in defeat. *I can't do it.* "Come home to me, then. I'm asking you to come home to me."

"Thank you." He kissed her one final time, lingered at her mouth. "I love you, beautiful girl. Always."

"I love you, too."

Then he was gone.

Chapter Six

Derek nodded as one of his officers sent him a signal from the warehouse across the street, one of their many surveillance vantage points. In a matter of minutes, they would move in on the meeting. They'd coordinated with the SWAT team and narcotics department, all of them with an interest in bringing down the two crime families supplying illegal drugs and weaponry to Chicago's streets. In minutes, a department helicopter would arrive, giving the operation eyes above the warehouse in case anyone inside tried to flee the scene. Moments to go until their carefully orchestrated plan came together. Then he'd give the signal for his men, SWAT, and narcotics officers to converge on the meeting.

Based on surveillance reports and the informant they currently had in custody, over a hundred members of the Lazio and Modesto crews were taking part in the covert meeting. They were all armed and under orders to provide cover if needed for the higher-ranking members to escape. Lazio included. His men, the other departments, they were aware of the risks and were just as dedicated to the cause as Derek. He reminded himself he'd planned for every eventuality. He'd done everything possible to safeguard his officers. This was everything he'd worked for and soon, one way or another, it would be over.

He didn't want to be distracted. This operation demanded his full attention. Today he would have justice for a fallen officer. Possibly prevent numerous deaths in the future, deaths of officers and citizens alike. Yet it couldn't be helped. His thoughts continued to stray to Ginger. To her broken expression as she demanded he put her out of her misery and... Derek couldn't finish the thought. Couldn't think about the conclusion she'd drawn without feeling actual, physical pain lance through him. He'd hurt her. Made her question his commitment to her.

His decision to keep her in the dark had been a mistake. That much had become clear immediately. How could he have been such a hypocrite? He'd spent the last year earning her trust, reiterating the importance of having no secrets between them. Then when given the chance to prove how strong their bond had become, he'd left her to twist in the wind. God, just knowing she'd spent the week thinking he was drifting away made him feel ill. What would he have done if Ginger didn't come home for days on end? If she refused to talk to him? Derek knew exactly what he would do. Pin her down and love her, kiss her, reassure her until she opened up. He hadn't given her that chance. He'd hid like a coward, afraid to reveal his own fear.

Now, his fears consisted of something else entirely. He needed to return to her at all costs. Fixing the mess he'd made was imperative. He'd promised her. A broken promise couldn't be the memory he left her with. He simply wouldn't allow it.

With a minute to go before the helicopter arrived, tipping off the perpetrators inside the warehouse to their presence, a flashback hit him. Ginger running down the hospital corridor in a nightshirt and cowboy boots, hair streaming behind her. Launching herself into his arms. Under the false impression that he'd been shot, she'd raced to the hospital in the middle of the night and found him safe and sound, merely waiting for an injured officer to be released. It had marked the first time she'd freely admitted to her feelings. He'd vowed never to take those feelings for granted. And he had. He fucking had.

Moving images smothered him then. Ginger, pissed-off and gorgeous, giving him hell for acting jealous. Ginger, sleepy-eyed and smiling, gasping as his hand slipped between her legs. Ginger, dancing and laughing at one of his officers' weddings, looking so beautiful and happy it broke his heart and made it swell at the same damn time.

When he got out of this alive—because his promise left no other option—he was going to marry her. Before he did anything else. It suddenly felt like a goddamn sin that he hadn't done it before now. If he'd corrected the travesty before this, maybe she wouldn't have had room to let misgivings creep in. Maybe he wouldn't be terrified over the prospect of something happening to him, leaving her with nothing. No rights as his wife. In his heart, she already was his wife. He needed it to be official, so badly it burned in his chest.

The dull roar of helicopter rotors beat in the distance, signaling the start of their operation. Derek nodded at the officer stationed in the warehouse window across the street, who immediately raised a radio to his mouth.

This is it. Now or never.

With a heavy heart, Derek reminded each image of Ginger how much he loved them all. How he wished he had handled everything differently this week. He prayed she could somehow hear him. Then he determinedly tucked her safely away and moved into the warehouse, his men following close behind.

...

Ginger lay on her side, face pressed to the wooden floor. She'd been in the same position, facing the door since late last night. Waiting for Derek to walk through. At first she'd been a whirlwind of nervous energy. She'd pulled out her hefty reserve of magazines and started cutting. Several pieces, expensive ones she'd earmarked for future projects, were now covered in the fruits of her furious labor. She barely remembered a single second.

At one point, she'd considered turning on the news, but had immediately discarded the idea. She'd ignored phone calls from Patti. Willa. No news was better than bad news, to her way of thinking. The more time she'd had to think, the reasons behind Derek's action had begun to take shape in her mind and allowed for one dreaded conclusion. He wouldn't have kept the case a secret from her if it hadn't been incredibly dangerous. They did not keep things from each other. How many times had he drummed that fact into her head until she finally started believing it?

In order for Derek to keep her in the dark, his life had to be at risk. As soon as she'd realized that, she'd been unable to think of anything else. So she'd dropped her scissors into the pile of magazine scraps and lain down, her hand resting on her belly protectively. She didn't move a muscle for fear she'd break apart and cease to exist. As the morning light illuminated the apartment, she wished fervently for the darkness to return. Everywhere the sunlight touched was another memory sent to haunt her. Ginger could practically hear his deep voice echoing through the apartment.

"Baby, you're making us late again."

Ginger smiled behind their bedroom door. They'd been on their way to a department ceremony in which Derek would be honored by the commissioner for his role in a drug sting earlier that year. "I'm always worth the wait, though, darlin'."

"Can't argue with that."

She'd yelped when the bedroom door swung open, royal-blue dress halfway down her body. "Derek, knock it off. I'm almost ready. You're just going to distract me." He'd run his hands up her thighs, over her bottom. "The hell with it. Let's stay here."

"No." Her protest had been breathless. "You deserve this ceremony. You worked hard and earned it. We're going."

Derek had picked her up and plunked her down on the dresser. His mouth moved over hers sweetly, long enough to turn her bones to jelly, before he'd pulled back. "We'll go. But only so I can see you smiling up at me from the front row. Proud of me." Fingers brushing over her cheek. "If I didn't have you sitting there in the audience, the honor wouldn't mean a damn thing."

"I'm always proud of you," she'd whispered back, shaken by his words. "So proud."

He'd cleared his throat and looked away, still getting used to his own feelings, she'd mused. She'd understood the sentiment too well. "Good. Then move that beautiful ass." She'd laughed and let him carry her out of the bedroom over his shoulder without a single word of protest.

The memory faded just as she heard the sound of a key turning in the lock. Ginger slowly moved into a sitting position, positive her imagination was playing tricks on her. Then Derek walked in, looking filthy and exhausted, yet wonderful at the same time. His gaze found her and warmed. A loud sob tore from her throat. Sweet, cleansing relief cocooned her, chasing away the last of her worry. Yet on its heels came palpable frustration. It had been numbed by the fear until now, but the anger bred through helplessness wouldn't be held back any longer. She'd been left in agony for a week, unprepared because he'd wanted to be noble. A part of her knew the frustration was just anxiety leaving her body in a rush, but she couldn't help it. She needed to let it out. Make damn sure he never did this to her again.

"I've got something to say, Lieutenant, so you listen real well." She rose to her feet, went toward him, finger pointed squarely at his chest. "I doubted you, *us*, this week and I'm damn sorry about it. I'm still learning. I might keep on learning forever." Ginger dragged in a shuddering breath. "But you doubted us, too. You doubted *me*. You didn't give me enough credit to understand your job. How much it means to you. I *know*. I know everything about you, Derek Tyler. So, I'm sorry I messed up and lost sight of what's between us, but you messed up, too."

"You're right," he said abruptly, bringing her up short. "I didn't give you the chance to be strong enough for us both when you're the strongest person I know. I'm sorry."

Her heart thundered in her ears. His words were so unexpected, she couldn't process them. "Help me understand."

"It was bad, Ginger. I knew it would bad be going in." He released a pent-up breath, shifted on his feet. An action unlike her usually stoic Derek. "I couldn't say it out loud. I couldn't look at you and tell you I was putting myself in a high-risk situation. Not after I demanded you never do the same again." His gaze penetrated hers. "This was something I had to do. Something important. I'm sorry as hell I didn't share it with you. If something happens to one of us, the other suffers. I forgot it goes both ways. Until the last second."

Tears threatened to fall, but she determinedly held them back. "What happened?"

"We got Lazio. Crippled Modesto. Everyone is alive, but it was fucking close."

Relief, coupled with pride in Derek, blurred her vision. She looked up at him, hiding nothing, seconds from throwing herself into his arms and never letting go, but he'd become distracted by something behind her. An odd expression crossed his face. One she'd never seen before. With a frown, Ginger turned and looked at the furniture scattered around the living room, as though seeing it for the first time.

Pink. Baby. Shit. Everywhere. Chairs, nightstands, even lampshades were covered in carefully pasted and lacquered collages of rattles, pictures of babies, storks, smiling parents, bottles.

Ginger whirled back around to find Derek watching her, the intensity of his expression robbing her of any lingering frustration. She hadn't even needed to tell him. Without her saying a word, he'd known, known her habits enough to figure her secret out on his own. Still, she couldn't decipher how he felt about the news. His face gave nothing away.

"You're pregnant."

She placed a hand over her belly and nodded.

Derek inhaled shakily. "How long have you known?"

"Just this week."

Pain slashed across his features. "Oh, baby." He dropped to his knees in front of her, encircling her waist with his arms and pulling her close. His mouth moved over her belly, muttering gruff apologies that sent tears cascading down her cheeks. Throat tight, emotions rubbed raw, Ginger could only stroke his hair comfortingly. Every excruciating moment she'd experienced overnight fell away until all she cared about was taking away his pain. The guilt she knew he now harbored for shutting her out when she needed him most. It's what they did for each other. What she would always do, as long as he'd let her.

"You tried to tell me, didn't you? And I just walked out."

She reacted to the self-loathing in his voice by kneeling in front of him on the floor. "Derek, it's okay. You're here now."

Face paling of color, he sat back on his heels. "Last night

at the party, I...did I hurt anything? God, I didn't know—"

"No." She shook her head for emphasis. "That's the one good thing about having so much time on my hands this week. Lots of late nights Googling embarrassing-ass questions. Nothing we do together will ever hurt me. Or...the baby."

"The baby." Finally, he took her in his arms. She burrowed her face in his neck and breathed deeply. His chest rose and fell steadily beneath her. "Our baby."

Hope permeated her chest. "You're happy?"

His incredulous expression was like a healing balm. He sobered when he saw her drastic relief, appearing to realize just how worried she'd been over his reaction. Before she could blink, he'd scooped her off the floor and set her down on the dining room table. "Ginger, happy is a pitiful, inadequate word to describe what I'm feeling right now. This happened in Miami, correct?"

"I-I think so, yes. How did you—"

"How did I know? I didn't." He winked, brushed her mouth with his. "But I'd hoped like hell."

A laugh burst from her throat. It felt damned amazing. "You're unbelievable."

Derek kissed her again, deeper, longer. She swore she could feel it in her soul. "Ah, Ginger. If I could do this week over..."

"I wouldn't." She smoothed his arched brow with her thumb. "We're not perfect. We make mistakes and we always come out stronger on the other side. I hope we never stop screwing up."

He laughed softly. "Then we won't. Ever. Not if you say yes." Derek reached into his jacket pocket. "I should have been home hours ago, but jewelry stores don't open until ten in the morning. And I wasn't coming home without a ring." A black velvet box appeared between them in his palm. His lips quirked when she slapped a hand over her mouth. "Ginger

Peet, you were mine the moment I saw you not twenty yards from this spot. I need it to be permanent. I need to call you mine in every sense of the word. Give me that honor and I'll never give you a reason to doubt me ever again."

"Yes, Derek. *Yes.* Make me your wife." When he plucked her off the counter and spun her around, their laughter echoed through the apartment.

・・・

Derek leaned back against the rim of the bathtub, hot water soothing his tired, aching muscles. His eyes threatened to close, but he refused to lose sight of Ginger for even a moment. When she drew her nightshirt over her head to reveal her naked body and slipped into the water with him, Derek's exhaustion went on hiatus. Steam from the bath caused her hair to curl, her face to flush. It reminded him of the first time they'd been in this bathroom together. When he'd touched her smooth skin for the first time. Listened to her cry his name.

He drew her back against his chest. Having her so close forced the chaotic events of the previous night to recede into the background almost completely. Only she could do that. Still, his chest felt heavy. Images that didn't belong anywhere near her danced behind his eyes. They would likely never leave him. Remembering their earlier conversation about honesty, he shared his burden, instinctively knowing she would understand.

"I fired my gun last night. Several times." He swallowed hard. "I didn't have a choice."

Ginger let her head fall back onto his shoulder and looked him square in the eye. "Of course you didn't, Derek." She seemed to sense his lingering restlessness and pulled away to face him. He didn't need any more assurances from her.

Everything she felt was right there in her eyes, her complete faith in him already beginning to mend the damage. She took a sponge in her hand and lathered it with soap, cleaning his neck and throat before moving lower to his chest.

Derek wouldn't lie to himself. Sitting in his bathtub, being washed clean by the beautiful woman carrying his child...it made him feel like a fucking king. Damn, he'd needed this. Needed *her*. She knew it, too. He could see it in the way she bit her lip, looked up at him through those long eyelashes. She knew she ruled his entire world. That certainty made him so goddamn happy, he could barely draw air. And hell, of course, it turned him on.

He took the sponge from her hand, let it fill with water. Then he squeezed the moisture out over her breasts, loving the way her breath faltered, her nipples peaked. His gaze followed the path of water as it streamed down her body. "I can't wait until your belly starts to show. When I can walk down the street holding your hand, everyone knowing I put a baby inside you."

Her flush deepened. "Hmmm. This could be a very good thing." Smiling saucily, she turned in his lap, making him growl when her wet bottom slipped over his erection. "Maybe we've finally found a way to cure your jealousy, Lieutenant."

"I'll never be cured of my jealousy. Not now. Not in fifty years." He gripped Ginger's hips, worried her ear with his teeth. "And don't pretend for a second that you don't love it."

Her laughter rolled over him. "All right, I won't take issue with the green-eyed monster for now. On one condition." She guided his hard flesh to her entrance and sunk down, melting back onto his chest as he filled her to the hilt.

Derek tilted his hips, scorching heat and need spearing through him. Watching him over her shoulder through heavy-lidded eyes, Ginger dipped and swiveled, driving him insane. He groaned in surrender. "Name your condition. I'll agree to anything, baby. Just don't stop moving."

She didn't answer, merely continuing to ride him. Her pace increased steadily, pushing him past his breaking point, until his grip on her hips tightened and he was dragging her up and down his length, racing frantically toward release, Ginger's name a litany on his lips. It was too much. Her love stripped him bare until nothing else existed but them, in that place in time. He felt her come undone and followed quickly behind, pulling her back for a moaning kiss as they shook in the aftermath.

Long moments passed before Derek remembered Ginger's words. *On one condition.*

He wrapped her in his arms. "Name your condition, beautiful girl."

She placed his hand over her belly. "If it's a girl, we name her Dolly."

Derek's booming laughter ricocheted off the bathroom walls. He placed a gentle kiss on her shoulder. "Dolly it is."

Acknowledgments

To Heather Howland for texting me with this idea on a boring Wednesday afternoon. It could not have been a better way to put a button on Derek and Ginger's story for me, and hopefully for those who enjoyed meeting the couple in *Protecting What's His*.

To my husband, Patrick, for dropping off sandwiches and leaving without a word while I was unable to stop writing this story. And my daughter, Mackenzie, for being a bright, beautiful ball of inspiration.

Lastly, to the readers who loved Derek and Ginger enough to make this novella a possibility—especially Bailey's Babes—thank you a zillion times.

About the Author

New York Times and USA TODAY bestselling author Tessa Bailey lives in Brooklyn, New York, with her husband and young daughter. When she isn't writing or reading romance, she enjoys a good argument and thirty-minute recipes.

www.tessabailey.com
Join Bailey's Babes!

Discover the Line of Duty series...

ASKING FOR TROUBLE
PROTECTING WHAT'S HIS
HIS RISK TO TAKE
OFFICER OFF LIMITS
STAKING HIS CLAIM

Also by Tessa Bailey

UNFIXABLE
BAITING THE MAID OF HONOR
OWNED BY FATE
EXPOSED BY FATE
DRIVEN BY FATE
RISKIER BUSINESS
RISKING IT ALL
UP IN SMOKE
CRASHED OUT
BOILING POINT
RAW REDEMPTION
THROWN DOWN
WORKED UP
WOUND TIGHT

Enjoy more heat from Entangled...

ONE NIGHT STAND AFTER ANOTHER
a novel by Amanda Usen

Clara Duke lives to crochet wearable art. But right this second, she's looking at the one guy who has the uncanny ability to unravel her in every possible way. *Zane Brampton*. A whole night with this delectable, gorgeous man would be nothing less than a total sexpocalypse. But then Zane wants his chance to prove he deserves more than one night...and he might just be the thread that snaps all of Clara's perfectly crocheted plans.

A SWEET SPOT FOR LOVE
a novel by Aliyah Burke

Former pro baseball player Linc Conner knows exactly where his head's at. But when it comes to single mom Emma Henricksen, Linc can't see straight. Emma's too busy raising her gifted little girl to have a sex life that's not battery-operated. Still, how could she resist being engaged to a guy who's the sexual equivalent of her favorite dessert, even if it's just pretend? Now it's a game with a whole lot of chemistry between the guy who's used to playing the field—and the woman who opted out of the game long ago. All that's missing is one helluva curveball...

Playing It Tough
a Sydney Smoke Rugby novel by Amy Andrews

Cosmetic tattoo artist Orla Stewart went from being the ultimate party animal to living a life that's ridiculously straight and narrow. Turns out, cancer can change a girl. A lot. Until one very hot, very unwelcome intruder turns things upside down. American rugby import Ronan Dempsey needs to clean his act up, and the pool house belonging to a family friend is the perfect place to hideaway. The chemistry is instantaneous, charged, and absolutely, completely, totally off-limits. Now it's a deliciously torturous game of pushing boundaries and holding out. It's just a matter of time before someone breaks...

Printed in Great Britain
by Amazon